Neighborhood Adventures

of Minnee, Genie Boy, Terri

And Their Unspoken Truth

Lola Sapphire

Life Chronicles Publishing
Give your life a voice!
lifechroniclespublishing.com
ISBN-13: 978-1-950649-04-4
Cover Design: Shakyena Sterling
Editor: Jada Berteaux
Life Chronicles Publishing Copyright © 2019

Contents

Dedication

To my Great-grandfather, who told me countless stories when I sat in the kitchen with him as a child. Thank you for passing the mantle of storytelling to me.

CHAPTER ONE

MEETING GRANDMAMA

Mama gripped a handkerchief between her two hands and periodically dabbed her tear-stained face. Uncle's left arm draped around her as he stared into space; his eyes were sad and heavy. My little sister cuddled Mama's left arm in distress, and my brother was sitting to the right of me looking out the window. We were in a black limousine with tinted windows on our way to the funeral. We parked on the driveway side of Tabernacle Missionary Baptist Church. My uncle opened the door first and went out, then Mama, my sister, and I, and lastly my brother. We remained in place for a moment until a man dressed in black with white gloves guided us through the opened door. Afterward, double doors opened, slowly held by two people who were also dressed in black with white gloves. We were directed to sit in the front row. I didn't recognize many of the faces of the members of the congregation. I asked my brother, "Whose funeral?"

"Grandmama's," he answered.

Whose Grandmama? I wondered.

The service ended quickly, and it was time to view the deceased. We all stood, and my heartbeat raced in my ears. Slowly, one person at a time looked at her, cried and moved on. As I walked up to the casket I stopped and looked at her tiny face dotted with freckles and shaped by reddish-brown hair. To me, she looked as though she was asleep. Her name was Gloria Williams Stocker and her funeral was our first meeting.

CHAPTER TWO

THE UNEXPECTED MOVE

Mama, my brother, sister and I lived in Creston Hills on the eastside of Oklahoma City. We lived in a three-bedroom duplex where the driveway went straight to our house. We lived there for over a year and Mama worked as a kitchen helper at a hospital. I'd just graduated from sixth grade a few days before; it was a time of happiness. Mama's boyfriend wasn't around, and that was calming.

Then my siblings and I, without Mama, moved to my uncle's house northeast of the city. His place was on the two hundredth block of Twelfth Street. A two-story brick building with four apartments down and four upstairs. We were going to be living on the second floor. The apartment was large with two windows straight to the back. I noticed, to the far left of the kitchen, a place to eat. In the back of the kitchen was another place to sit and eat. Immediately to the left of the kitchen was a large bathroom and to the right was a small bedroom. All of us would be sleeping in the living room; that would remain our sleeping space until Mama returned.

My uncle told me that Mama went to jail for writing *hot* checks and that she would return in a month. I didn't feel anything after listening to him; I was no fan of his. He and Mama weren't the best of friends either; he just stepped back into our lives after years of absence.

CHAPTER THREE
GENIE BOY

The following day I went outside. As I stepped off the wide porch, I saw children laughing, running, falling and playing in our front yard and in the neighbor's yard. It was a warm day, and it felt good to hear laughter. I began walking down the path of the sidewalk and stopped. I saw two boys on bikes. They looked about my age.

"Are you new here?" One of the riders asked.

"Yeah," I replied.

"Where you from?" he asked growing more animated.

"The Eastside."

"I'm Genie Boy, and this is Terri," he said with a grin. "What's your name?"

"Minnee."

"Ya'll live here now?" Genie Boy asked.

"No! This is my uncle's house." I answered irritated by *that* question.

Then he asked, "You wanna walk around?"

"Sure!" I said thinking this was a way to see a part of this place with someone who knew it. Although I agreed, I walked slowly and purposefully.

We made our way up Twelfth Street to the corner and took a left turn toward 13th. As we neared 13th Street, we passed a tavern on the left. It was part of an extended building painted a sickly greenish blue color. The door, the same color as the building, was wide open and light escaped from the backdoor creating a tunnel effect. Glass mirrors were on the wall behind the long counter and faded numbers hung crookedly above the door opening. Next, we passed a barbershop and stopped in the parking lot of a record store.

"They play music outside sometimes when the summer comes," Genie Boy informed me.

"Where?" I asked looking around the empty parking lot.

He pointed upward saying, "Up there!"

I looked up and saw a speaker that was fixed on the left side of the door. It looked like a loudspeaker, the kind that was mounted outside the back of my school in Creston Hills. I looked across the street and saw something huge that looked like a metal beehive. I pointed, "What's that?"

Genie Boy said, "That's an old cement place."

"How do you know?" I questioned him.

"Cause, we went there before," Terri chimed in. "You wanna go?"

"No," I shouted.

"You wanna go to the store then?" Genie Boy asked.

"Where?"

"Back there," he said pointing in the direction behind us."

"Sure!"

The store had pretty much everything I needed. I loved hot pickles, barbeque potato chips, hot link sandwiches, and Nehi Grape soda. This place was an oasis for me. There was a parking lot out front with just a few spaces for cars to park.

A little girl, maybe nine or so, stomped up to Genie Boy and said, "Mama said come home!"

"Ok, I'm comin' soon." He turned to me and asked, "You wanna walk back to your uncle's?"

"Yeah."

His sister yelled, "Mama said now I'm tellin' you!" as she stomped back across the street.

After they walked me back, I sat on my uncle's front porch for a while just thinking about my day's adventures.

My sister walked up to me, just coming from the apartment house which was about two doors down.

"Minnee, come here let me show you somethin' over there."

"What do you want?"

"Come and see," she coaxed me.

The building that was two doors down from where we lived was vacant. We walked up to the porch and stepped inside the apartment. It looked the same as where we lived. Inside the building smelled of old cigarettes. I walked up the staircase leading to the second floor and down the hall in front of me was a window with tattered curtains that looked as if a wild cat had shredded them. As we opened the door, children of all ages were jumping and running around in the room. They were even jumping on the mattress that was flat on the floor in a closet.

The room was filled with all types of furniture; a chest of drawers and a mirror that sat between it and a stool. Two perpendicular windows were in the room; one with a faded window shade, the other with curtains that looked like hanging strings. I sat on the stool and looked in the drawers. While the kids were jumping, something caught my eye. There was a girl who might have been a little older than I was. She was jumping as much as some of the others, but when she jumped her blouse lifted half-way up and her stomach pushed out; it pushed out like a basketball. She was pregnant! Just as fast as I noticed. My sister redirected my attention.

"You wanna look around over there?" as she pointed to another room across the hall.

"You wanna go back to the house?" I asked her in reply.

"No, not yet," she said.

"I'm goin' back," I told her as my feet marched to our front porch where I sat and again took up deep thought.

CHAPTER FOUR

IRON WOMAN

Some say my little sister, Alice, was a *tomboy*. She could leap a fence with a single bound and throw just about any boy or girl down with little effort. I remembered one day when we lived in Creston Hills, my sister fought six out of eight kids in one family. I don't know how it all started, but Mama yelled from the kitchen window, "Who is Alice fighting out there?" She ran outside to the front yard, and I jumped up and went out after her. My sister had knocked down three kids already while another walked up to her swinging. The mother of the other kids stood nearby in the middle of the street.

"There won't be no double teamin' my daughter," Mama yelled.

The woman crossed her arms as she shifted from one foot to the other. My sister dipped and hit the kid straight in the nose. He ran to his mama, and another came at full speed toward her. She shifted her body, stuck out her foot and tripped the girl who then also fell to the ground. The last kid she fought stood with her toe to toe. Somehow, Alice swooped around with a half Nelson and grabbed the girl around her neck and flung her down, too.

Alice turned around to Mama and said, "Mama, I'm tired."

"This fight is over," Mama said. And just like that the woman and her children walked back toward their house. Alice went inside the house to our room and fell fast asleep. At that time, she was eight-years-old and later, she would be donned "Iron Woman."

During our time with my uncle, I didn't see my little sister often and I saw my brother even less. When the sun came up they both hit the ground running. Particularly Bruce; he was a shadow, but he came home every evening. When his friends found out his middle name was Wayne, they called him *Bat Man*. Probably why he was such a phantom. My uncle wasn't known for checking on us, we pretty much had our own barometers. I was more of a homebody but in no hurry to go upstairs into his apartment. I didn't have much of a relationship with him and it didn't improve after he kept us.

CHAPTER FIVE

I GUESS WE LOST SOMEBODY

My mama and her on-again-off-again boyfriend were yelling at each other outside in the alleyway that night. Mama was on her way to the club, all of a sudden, I heard loud bumping sounds. Our place on the edge of the alley was where the sounds originated. Mama came back to the house, and she looked horrifying. She had been beaten so much that her face looked like it had been slammed into the wall many times. One eye was swollen and shut, and the other not far off. Her nose was clogged with blood, mouth swollen and she had a split upper lip. Four lumps rested across her forehead and her clothes were torn and hardly on her body. She was all of five foot eight and 100 pounds soaking wet.

"Minnee, get me that stack of newspapers from over there!" she yelled towards me.

I ran to the front room and picked up as many newspapers as I could handle. She said, "Drop them!"

I dropped the stack next to her. In one sweep, Mama had swept all the covers off the bed and said, "Hurry up and help me lay out these papers on the bed."

Next, she climbed slowly onto the bed, frowning as she covered herself, "Look in the drawer over there. Get a piece of paper and pen."

I gave her the paper and pen.

"Go to Anna's house and call your grandpa. Tell him to hurry!"

I ran to Anna's and called Granddaddy George.

"Hi, Granddaddy, Mama's hurt. She said come."

"What's wrong, Minnee?"

"Mama's hurt. She's bleeding."

"I'm coming," he said hanging up the phone with a clash.

I went back and told Mama, "Granddaddy said he's coming."

Mama looked worried, scared and groaned in pain. I sat down close to her on the edge of the bed. Tears streamed down my face, and I started to cry hard. I was confused. Wondering *why did he hurt her like that? Why does she stay with him?"* I was sad and mad at the same time. Granddaddy rushed in the house looking frightened.

"Minnee, go back to the neighbor's house and call the ambulance."

I ran back to Anna's, "Miss Anna, I need to call the operator; Mama needs to go to the hospital."

"Please send an ambulance, I cried into the telephone."

"What's your address? Ma'am, what's your address?"

"Minnee, what's she sayin'?" Anna asked anxiously.

"Address."

"Give me the phone. You get back home to your mama."

I ran back to the house. When I walked in, I saw one of the most shocking things of my life. A gigantic amount of blood covered a large space on the newspapers. There were bits of something within the blood. The odor was wet and heavy, like the smell of raw meat. It was Mama's blood and something else in it. I'll never forget what I saw; it was etched in my mind, heart and soul.

"Minnee, go call your uncle, here's his number," Granddaddy said handing me a crumpled paper.

By the time I got back, Granddaddy had managed to get the bloody matter wrapped in newspapers into a few garbage bags. Mama sat on the chair next to the bed, pale as a ghost and wrapped in covers exposing only her face. Two ambulance drivers came in and Mama walked slowly out the door with them. Not much longer, my uncle rushed in and helped Granddaddy clean up what was left. My uncle agreed to watch us until Mama returned from the hospital. I was told by Mama later that she had a miscarriage.

I guessed we lost somebody.

The next day, Granddaddy George brought a box full of different types of meats; he was a butcher. In the box was a whole chicken, ground beef, pan sausage, bacon, lunchmeat, cube steaks, and the works. What my uncle did the next day was cold blooded. He sat right in front of us at that kitchen table at breakfast and ate our food. He ate pancakes, at least three over easy eggs, about four slices of bacon and coffee. We ate cereal. He ate that food as if he was eating alone; As if we didn't exist. Scarfing food in his mouth like a shovel. Right then I knew he was not cool. When Mama returned, I told her everything. I didn't forget what he did to us.

CHAPTER SIX

BABYSITTING

I sat on the porch and felt sick to my stomach. I didn't notice my sister come up to me, "I'm hungry" she said.

"Girl stop scaring me like that! You wanna sandwich?"

"Yeah."

After we ate peanut butter and jelly sandwiches, my uncle's girlfriend asked, "You wanna babysit?"

I replied, "Yeah, who?"

"A friend of mine's son."

"When does she want me to babysit?" I asked.

"Tomorrow. She's paying two dollars."

She gave me the address to the two hundredth block of Thirteenth Street.

The next day, I walked to the lady's place. It was another brick building and the apartment was on the second floor. I knocked on the door and the lady opened the door holding a small boy probably about six years old. After she put Sam down and stepped aside, I walked in. She asked, "Hey, how are you?"

"Fine, Ma'am" I answered.

She said, "This is Sam. And your name is Minnee?"

"Yes, Ma'am."

"I just need your help for one day. We are leaving in two days, going back home."

"Yes, Ma'am."

"You better listen, Sam, you hear me?" she directed the little boy.

He said, "Yes, Ma'am."

"Oh, here's the key." She handed me a little silver tarnished house key.

Sam and I left the building and crossed the street. I heard a song playing from the record shop. It was Aretha Franklin, *"I never loved a man the way that I love you,"* she sang. I knew that song in my sleep because Mama played that song over and over and over. We turned the corner onto Twelfth and when we got closer, I saw Genie Boy, Terri and another boy.

"Hey, Minnee, you wanna go to the underpass?" Genie Boy shouted.

"What's that?" I asked never having heard talk of that spot before.

"Let me show you."

The three mounted their bikes alongside Sam and me, and we walked back toward the record shop. Before we reached the corner of Thirteenth, I heard another song.

"Y'all hear that?" I asked them.

Terri said, "Yeah, they playin' music now."

"What's that song?" I asked them.

Genie Boy and Terri in unison said, "I dunno."

The music and song was by Archie Bell and the Drells.

"I ain't heard that song before," I said puzzled by the tune.

"It must be new," Genie Boy guessed.

I remembered some of the words, *Let's tighten it up now. Do the tightening up. Everybody can do it now.*

We turned left and on the next block, the street sloped downward and train tracks crossed the top over a short bridge.

"Hey, train tracks" I said excitedly. "I be hearin' the train at night, but they sound so far away."

Genie Boy said, "You wanna jump one?"

"No, those trains go too fast."

"Not over there," he said as he pointed to a breezeway with buildings on both sides of the train tracks. "It slows down when the train passes through there."

"Oh!" I said.

"You still wanna go?"

"I dunno."

Terri said, "It's a lot of fun. Don't be scared."

Sam and I continued to walk down under the overpass and walked up the incline. When we reached the top of the corner, we stopped.

Genie Boy pointed and said, "Look over there. That place is called the Capital."

"That place is called what?"

"Yeah, funny huh?" he laughed.

"What you mean?"

He said, "I dunno. It just seems funny to me."

Gary, the other boy said, "It's the place where the government is. You know the mayor and stuff."

"Who is he?" I asked.

"I'm hungry," Sam said interrupting our conversation.

"Ok, you wanna go back to your house and get somethin' to eat?" I asked the little boy.

"Yeah," he said quietly.

"Don't you still wanna go on the train tomorrow?" Genie Boy was determined.

"I dunno yet" I told him. "I'll let you know later."

"It's fun," Terri chuckled. "We can help you."

Genie Boy and Gary pedaled back under the overpass.

Terri yelled, "Genie Boy, wait up." Genie Boy yelled back, "You dragging."

Sam and I started walking back to his house when I saw a big yellow bus pass us. I saw a few letters on the side of it, N-A-Z-A-R. We kept walking up the sidewalk, got to his place, walked upstairs, and I opened the door. We went to the kitchen. The only two things in the icebox was a half loaf of light bread and a small bottle of Catsup. I opened the freezer section which, back in the day, was a small compartment with a small door covering it and inside that part was mostly ice. I could see part of what looked like a pack of ground beef. I looked in the kitchen drawers and found an ice pick. I picked away at the ice and tugged at the pack of meat until it finally gave way. I thawed it out with cold water in the sink. I found a skillet and fried the meat. We ate ground beef sandwiches.

Walking back to Twelfth, another song played by Aretha Franklin, *You better think, think, think. Think about what you're trying to do to me, yeah. Think, think, think.*

Mama loved Aretha Franklin and I did, too. She played another song called, *Respect. R-E-S-P-E-C-T take care of T.C.B.* I often wondered what T. C.B. meant.

We made it to my uncle's, and I saw my little sister.

"You wanna go buy something from the donut store?" she asked me.

I said, "Where you get some money from?"

"Miss Mary."

"Who's Miss Mary?" I wanted to know who this new person was.

"I met her a few days ago. I like her. Do you wanna go?"

She looked at Sam and said, "Who's this?"

"Sam. I'm babysitting him."

"Do you wanna go?" she repeated.

"Sure!" I finally said.

We all walked down about half a block to the Hostess bread outlet store. All kinds of bread and other stuff were inside, but my sister went straight to the cupcakes and pies.

"Whatcha want?' she asked.

"Will you get Sam something, too?"

With her back to me, she said, "Ok, only one thing right over here," as she made a circular motion with both arms toward that specific zone.

"Go ahead Sam and get something from over there," I told him.

Sam picked up a pack with two chocolate cupcakes. I did, too. My sister got chocolate cupcakes, a honey bun and an apple pie. Once we left the building, Genie Boy, Terri and Gary rode up to us.

"What y'all doin' here?" Terri asked.

My sister said, "Why?"

"I'm just asking."

"It ain't your business" Alice snapped and kept walking.

Genie Boy asked again about the train jump, "You thought about going with us tomorrow?"

"Not really, but I'll go."

"We're goin' downtown," Terri said.

"I'm not goin' that far," I told them.

Genie Boy said, "It's really close. You'll see."

We got back to my uncle's place, went upstairs and Sam's mama was there.

"I'm glad you are back. It's time to go, Sam. Oh, here's your two dollars. Thank you so much."

"You're welcome, Ma'am."

"You got somethin' to say, Sam?"

"Bye, I had a lot of fun," Sam said on cue as they walked out the door.

CHAPTER SEVEN

THE CHARACTERS

Later, my phantom brother, Bruce, came through the door, he had what looked like dried pie on his face. It looked like he'd partially wiped it off.

"What happened to you? What's that stuff all on your face?" I asked him with a disgusted look on my own face.

"I was at the fair?"

"What fair?" I demanded to know.

"It's on the other side of town. I got some money for it, too."

He pulled out ten dollars.

"Who did you go with?"

"Me and a friend. Do you wanna go to the store? I'll buy you something."

"Ok," I said quickly.

My brother and I walked to the store, and he bought Mike & Ike candy, barbeque chips and Hi-C Orange soda. I got barbeque chips and Nehi grape soda. When we came out of the store, Bruce saw his friend and ran across the street to him, and they cut across the grass on Eleventh and disappeared.

Genie Boy and Gary rolled up and Genie Boy asked me, "Is that your brother?"

"Yeah. Where's Terri? He sticks to you like glue?"

"He got in trouble with Mama."

I noticed my little sister, Alice, across the street with an odd- looking woman.

"Ain't that your sister over there?" Genie Boy said tilting his head in her direction.

"Yeah. Who's that lady she's with?"

"That's Miss Mary. They call her a bag lady cause she's always diggin' in the garbage. Why is your sister with her?" Genie Boy quizzed with a confused stare.

"My sister said she likes her, and they find stuff."

Before we finished our conversation, a man passed us. He was wearing tan looking pants, a white tank top tucked into his pants and a black belt. He wore gold house shoes except the toes of the house shoes which were curled up like genie shoes, and it looked like he had black nylon socks or something on, too.

"Who's that?"

"They call him Miss Eddie," Genie Boy told me.

Miss Eddie walked a little past us and snapped, "That's my name. Don't wear it out!" He went switchin' down the street.

"You wanna go to the record shop?"

Genie Boy asked unfazed by Miss Eddie.

"Yeah."

We crossed the street on Twelfth and started toward Thirteenth. To the left of us, believe it or not, Genie Boy's sister was sitting on top of a table in the neighborhood tavern.

"Genie Boy, is that your sister in there?" I asked in shock.

"Yeah."

"How old is she?"

"Nine."

"You trippin'? Nine? Is she going to get in trouble being there?" I questioned him and could not hold back my disbelief.

"Probably not cause Mama's in there, too. Vivian be doin' too much. She don't listen to me. She mostly tries to get me in trouble."

We reached the record shop and went in. Miss Eddie was in there, too, and she was giving us the mean eye. The record shop had LPs, 45s, incense, and air fresheners for cars. There were posters with black backgrounds, neon paintings of men and women with Afros and peace symbols in almost all of them. They were called blacklight posters because they glowed in the dark. We looked around while the song, *I Got the Feelin'* by James Brown played. Looking through the LPs, I remembered last summer when we went way out to the country. We were with Grandpa and Grandma Bailey. They lived in a house without running water and had an outhouse for a toilet. It was so much fun. The Bailey's had a little white church on their land, too. We spent a lot of time in there. Grandpa Bailey really knew how to play the guitar or at least it sounded good. Another man played the bass and there was a drummer, too. One day, my brother and his friend, Tony, made a challenge. It was who could swivel his leg down the middle aisle of Grandpa Bailey's church like James Brown to the front aisle. Grandpa's church looked like a small white house. The gospel music they played was loud and the rhythm moved the soul. With the three-person instrumentation, they started at the very back of the church in the middle aisle. They took off swivel legs and all. Once they hit midway the aisle, Tony lifted and held onto the top edge of his pants. He raised his left leg and he swiveled his right leg down to the front row of the church. He left my brother in the dust.

"They got the Holy Spirit!" Grandpa shouted.

They had the spirit all right. The spirit of James Brown.

Genie Boy asked me, "What's your favorite song?"

"I think it's called Tighten Up?"

"Who is it by?"

Gary spoke up, "Archie Bell & the Drells. Archie came from a place called Houston and they got their start with a DJ called Frazier."

"How you know all of that?" I asked him.

Gary said, "My uncle told me."

"What's your favorite song, Gary?" I asked.

"Cold Sweat. What about you, Genie Boy?"

"Soul Man." Are you ready to go now?"

We left the record shop but when we turned and walked toward Twelfth, I noticed someone lying down on the grass side of the sidewalk. As we got closer, Genie Boy ran up and fell to his knees. It was his mama. She had thrown up, and it covered most of her dress. He was talking to her as she swatted him away. He raised her slowly as she stumbled now and then. He walked with her as she staggered with his assistance. Gary and I walked slowly with them until I reached Twelfth and went home.

CHAPTER EIGHT

HERE COMES THE TRAIN

It was noon the next day and I looked out the window and saw the three of them, Genie Boy, Terri and Gary, outside. I walked out to the front porch.

"Hey, ready to go?" Genie Boy yelled as he spotted me.

"As ready as I'm gonna get."

We started walking toward the Hostess outlet store, as we passed it about a half of a block down, there was a long opening with buildings on both sides. The train tracks went straight down the middle. When I turned and looked to the right, I noticed the overpass a little way off.

I glanced at Terri and noticed under his right eye a purplish mark. My stomach shivered. I'd seen bruises like that before.

"Here's what you need to do," Genie Boy interrupted my thoughts. "Watch the train car with open doors and start runnin' a little. Next, you have to jump and use half your body to get on. I'll pull you up. Ok?"

I said, "That's a lot."

"I'll help you, too. Remember watch for the train car with open doors."

Terri pointed saying, "Here it comes! Here comes the train!"

Genie Boy, Gary and Terri jumped on the train car like pros. I ran a little, jumped and both my hands caught splinters from the scratchy wood. Genie Boy did help me up though. I sat down and looked at my hands. "I got splinters in both my hands now," I complained. We all sat there quietly for a moment.

"We are gettin' closer to downtown, so we have to jump off," Genie Boy warned.

"We have to what?"

"It's not that hard. When you jump, just bend your knees a little," Genie Boy instructed me.

Terri asked, "Do you know how to jump and roll?"

I looked at him and said, "Are you kiddin'?" Terri laughed so hard.

Genie Boy said, "Ok, get ready to jump! You go first."

I jumped and tried to bend my knees, but my left ankle hurt a little after I jumped.

"Are you alright?" Genie Boy asked with the slightest bit of concern.

"These doggone splinters hurt way more than my ankle." I limped as they walked around the building opening.

We reached a movie theater and went in. The interior was loud with red-colored carpet, walls and counter area.

"Do you wanna go see the movie?" Genie Boy asked mischievously.

"What are you talkin' about?"

"I know how we can go see the movie. Let me show you."

I followed them as we made a left down the block, made another left and still another left into an alleyway. We stopped at an exit door.

"Let's go in here. Come on," Genie Boy beckoned the group.

We ducked down and sat on the first row. By that time my hands and ankle were throbbing. I was freaked out about the movie attendant. Sure enough, an attendant came in from the front entrance behind us with a flashlight, but luckily, not many people were in there. He turned around and went back into the lobby. I didn't even remember the movie. All I knew was that I was finished with them for that day.

"I'm ready to go home."

"Ok, let's go," Genie Boy complied.

As I limped my way up the alley, Terri asked, "Are we goin' on the train again?"

"No! I'm not doin' that no more. I'm limpin' like crazy and you talkin' bout jumpin' a train. Get real!"

They slowed their pace for me as we continued to walk back. I thought back to that old school bus the other day. I wanted to know more about it.

"When Sam and me was goin' back to his place, I saw a big ol' yellow bus. I saw it a few times. It had letters on it, N-A-Z-A. I don't remember no more."

Gary said, "That's the Nazarene bus; they drive around here in the summer."

"What else do they do?"

"They take you to something called Big Tent Revival, and you can eat, too."

"Have you ever been?" I stared at Genie Boy.

"Yeah, once or twice."

"You wanna go?" Terri asked.

Gary's voice trickled in, "When do they come back?"

Terri told us that the bus was there on Saturdays. Somebody said, "Let's go!" and we walked back more blocks than I cared to. I was extremely happy to get back to the house. I picked out as many splinters as I could and poured alcohol on my sore hands. I ripped a sleeping shirt of mine and wrapped my ankle until my left foot went numb. Thinking over it all, I had the best time ever. Jumping on that train with all of them was so cool.

CHAPTER NINE

BIG TENT REVIVAL

I heard some people talking outside, looked out the window, and it was Genie Boy, Gary and Terri outside waiting. This time my little sister went with us to the Nazarene Big Tent Revival. I convinced her to go, especially since we would get to eat some food.

"Hey, y'all, this is my sister, Alice. Alice this is Genie Boy, Terri and Gary." She didn't respond but just glared at them.

"I saw you at the bread store," Terri said in his friendly way.

"So, I saw you, too. Can we go now?"

We started walking up the street, made a left at the corner and walked to the parking lot of the record store. The song, *Tighten Up* was playing.

"Who's that playin'?"

My little sister demanded an answer and of course Gary spoke up, "Archie Bell & the Drells."

"I like that song."

There were other children and teens waiting for the big yellow bus, too as it pulled up from the slope and stopped just before our corner. A white man with a striped shirt and tan pants opened the flapped door as we filed in. We went straight to the back and sat down.

"What's a revival?" I didn't care who answered.

"I dunno," Gary said. "Just there's a lot of people and chairs to sit on and a circus tent."

"A circus tent? They got animals, too?" Alice was excited now.

"No. You sit under the tent, and chairs are lined up. And they play music and stuff."

"Minnee, you think it's gonna take a long time?" Alice whined.

"Why, you ain't got nowhere to go."

Terri started laughing.

"What's funny, Bugs Bunny?"

Terri stopped for just a moment and laughed again. Alice rolled her eyes and said, "Chump."

We pulled up to a place with a wide grassy area aside from a church a little way back. When we got out of the bus, Gary was right, there were a few big white tents. We went to the tent with rows of folding chairs lined up in long aisles. Genie Boy, Terri, Gary, Alice and I sat on the very last row.

Terri turned to me and asked loudly, "Do you smell that?"

"Everybody smell the food; it's back there." Alice turned in her chair to the back of us pointing toward the food. There was a big stage and people sitting on chairs at the back of the stage, too. Two things I clearly remember; the food and the man on the stage. He was a white man wearing a powdered blue prom style suit; his shirt even had ruffles down the middle of it. He had on shiny white shoes. Mama told me later that his shoes were patent leather. He talked loudly and screamed sometimes, too. This was the first time that I saw a white man scream like James Brown, but he did. He even wiped the sweat from his forehead. When he finished, people walked up to the stage, lined up, and that same man put his hand on their forehand and some fell down. It was as if they passed out or something. That was too wild, and I was glad it was over and time to eat! We lined up. There was so much food; chicken, pork chops, mashed potatoes, gravy, corn and green beans. We had more to pick from, and it was all good. We even had Kool-Aid, cake and pie for dessert. When we finished eating, we all stacked our plates. Soon after we finished with our meal, we were dropped off by the bus driver back to the same place where he picked us up. As I think back to this time, there were only two community outreach organizations that came to this neighborhood; the nuns and the Church of the Nazarene.

CHAPTER TEN

MAMA'S BACK

We all walked until we got to Twelfth, and Alice and I turned right and went to the house. When we went in, Mama was sitting on the couch.

"Mama! Mama, where you been? Alice cried hugging her. "You been gone for a long time."

Mama had been gone for about a month. She didn't come home that day when we lived on the Eastside. Granddaddy knocked on the door around three in the afternoon. I opened the door; he came in and told us to pack some clothes because Mama would be gone for a while. He told us that we would be going over to our uncle's place until she returned.

"Granddaddy, where's Mama at?" my brother asked.

"She'll tell you all when she sees you."

My sister returned to the living room, "Do I need my toothbrush?"

Granddaddy said, "Yes."

I felt sick to my stomach. This was the second time Mama had to leave but now she was back.

"I'm here now, baby. What y'all been doin?"

"We went on a big yellow bus and got somethin' to eat," Alice told her in a rush to get the reply out.

"It was the Church of Nazarene." I finished the story Alice had started. "They had somethin' called a Revival. Mostly a white man screaming with a prom suit on. The food was good though."

My uncle came through the door and said, "Hey, Pat, you out now?"

"Hey, Willie."

He said, "I've got some great news."

"What's that?"

"I got a job offer in San Francisco working at the San Francisco Chronicle."

"When are you leaving?"

"In two weeks."

Mama said, "Good! That gives me time to find a place."

"There are apartments available next to the record shop. You ought to check it out."

"I think I will."

Mama got a one-bedroom apartment upstairs. The apartment was furnished so that it wasn't so bad. The next day I overheard Mama and my uncle's girlfriend talking about going to California in a couple of months.

"I got my son back and need to save enough money to go to LA that way you guys can come after I find a place," I heard Anne say.

"Yeah, it's time to go. It's not easy to get started here," Mama seemed to really agree with the idea of moving.

"Willie is leaving next week, and I found an apartment up on 13th, a block up."

Two days later Genie Boy and Terri came over and we sat in the living room listening to James Brown when I heard a knock at the door. I opened it and there stood Vivian, Genie Boy's sister.

"Where's Genie Boy?"

"Right there," I told her pointing to him.

He got up from his spot and said, "Whatcha want?"

"Mama said come home and fix me somethin' to eat."

"Girl, I'm over here, wait a minute."

"I'm tellin' you and you gon' get in trouble, too."

"Are you gonna get in trouble?" I asked a little scared for him. "She looked mad."

Terri for once was speechless. Not much longer, we heard a pounding sound at the door. I opened the door and Genie Boy's mama and Vivian stood in the hallway. He stepped out the door to the left of me. Terri stood to the right of me with his back to the wall.

"Why didn't you come when Vivian came to get you? I sent her here to get you."

Just as fast as those words came from her mouth, she shot her fist straight to Genie Boy's nose. Like a bullet racing from its chamber at point blank range.   Blood sprayed from his nose and splattered my left cheek. The force was powerful enough to nearly lift her body from the floor. His mama stood all of four feet eight inches, maybe. The aftermath of his impacted nose drenched his shirt like the time a tailgate dropped on Mama's big toe and the buckle of water turned crimson in seconds. Genie Boy, Terri and I bowed our heads, maybe in shame.

"See I told you, you was gon' get in trouble." Vivian seemed almost tickled by the events.

"Get you motherfuckin' ass home now you son of a bitch."

He balled the bottom of his shirt and pressed it to his nose as they all left. I closed the door and slid down to the floor. Tears slowly fell from my eyes down my face. I walked into the bathroom, closed the door and looked in the mirror. His splattered blood was on my face. I need to get his blood off my face. *Why did she have to do that? Why?"*

I was sad and mad at the same time and my hands shook uncontrollably as I bowed my head to the sink and sobbed. My heart was sore, pummeled by life's pain filled score. I washed my face and went into the living room and sat down.

My sister ran into the living room really excited, then she stopped and said, "What's wrong with you?"

"Oh, nothing."

She looked at me suspiciously then said, "It's some nuns on the other side of here."

"What you mean nuns on the other side of here?"

She repeated her words, "It's three nuns in that driveway over there and they are gettin' ready to show some cartoons. Do you wanna come?"

I forced myself to stand, "Well, why not."

We both went through the kitchen out the back door where a wooden stairway had alternating flights of stairs going downward. When we arrived, sure enough, one nun was preparing the reel to reel projector which was on a steel cabinet with wheels. Another was positioning what looked to be a sheet over the garage door while hammering. The last nun was seated with three other children on blankets laid out on the driveway.

Alice moved to a spot and said, "Let's sit here."

I sat down next to her as she watched the Mickey Mouse cartoons. My mind was still back in the hallways. I couldn't believe what just happened a few hours ago. This was a great distraction, although I still felt devastated.

On our way back to the house, my sister said, "Do you know we are going to Los Angeles?"

"I remember Anne and Mama talkin' about somethin' like that."

"Yeah, me too I heard Mama talkin' to her. I think we are leaving soon."

"How soon is soon?" I wasn't sure how to feel about all of this moving stuff.

"I dunno," Alice replied with a quick shrug of her shoulders.

We entered through the back door of the kitchen. "Where have you two been?" Mama asked. She seemed slightly irritated.

"We was watching cartoons back over there by the garage. Three nuns showed us Mickey mouse cartoons," Alice said coyly.

"Mama, are we goin' to Los Angeles?" I blurted out.

"Yes, we are." She said stirring her instant coffee. "We should be leaving here in August."

August was two weeks away. *Wow*

"Anne wants you to babysit tomorrow night."

I was thinking about how to tell my new friends that we were going to Los Angeles.

"Yes, Ma'am."

CHAPTER ELEVEN

THE CADILLAC

I walked to Anne's apartment on Thirteenth Street on the 300th block. The building was another brick one, with five stairs made of concrete leading upward. On both sides of the stairs were cement railings that sloped upward. The railings were wide enough that one could sit on them or at least on an angle. At the bottom of the cement railings were two large concrete pots big enough to put flowers in. I walked through the door and slightly left was a flight of stairs and to the right a couple more stairs before finally walking up the last flight to the second floor. There was an apartment door to the left and Anne's place was to the right. I knocked on the door and she let me in. I sat on the couch close to the big window and Anne went back into the bathroom putting on makeup.

"There's lunch meat for sandwiches and chips on the table," she said from the bathroom. "Billy will be here soon for you to babysit him; he's with my sister. I also got your favorite soda. Don't you like Nehi grape soda?"

"Yes, Ma'am, Thank you."

There was knock at the door and Anne yelled, "Get the door, please."

When I opened the door, there was a girl who looked a little taller and older than I. She stood there for a moment. I smelled a familiar odor emanating from her. Her eyes were green but glassy and her hair looked light brown with looping curls. She had brown freckles on her face too.

Is Anne here?"

"Girl come on in," Anne said before I could reply.

I went back to the couch and sat a little to the right of the window. It was open and a nice evening breeze was blowing through. The older girl sat down on the far end of the couch. She dropped her purse between us. It was open, and I noticed two things. One, a big wad of money; it was the most money I'd ever seen. Two, a bottle of alcohol. The word on the bottle said, "Tanqueray" and the bottle looked almost empty.

"Anne, where are you going tonight?" The girl asked.

"Pat and me are going to the club Downtown."

While the two were continuing their conversation. I heard booming music coming from outside, so I looked out the window. All of a sudden, a big white car ran upon the sidewalk and slammed into the stairs. It hit the cement railing to the left which knocked one of the flowerpots off the railing to the ground. A man jumped from the car, lights on, music blasting and engine running. From what I could see, he was wearing a white suit, white shoes and a white hat, the car was white too with a drop top and white interior. *I learned later that the car was called a Cadillac Eldorado.* With a couple foot falls, the man pounded at the door, so hard that I jumped and moved toward the bathroom where Anne was.

"Open this door, Anne, I know you're in there! If you don't open this door, I'll knock it down!"

The girl said, "Let him in, I know what he wants."

Anne opened the door and the man pushed her to the side. The girl grabbed her purse and he snatched her up and threw her out the apartment. He lifted her and threw her down the flight of stairs. He walked down the stairs, stepped over her and kept walking to the car. Anne and I were standing just outside the door.

"Linda, are you alright?" Anne asked her in a panic.

She didn't respond but sat there for a moment and the man yelled, "Get your ass in this car."

She got up slowly and staggered to the car. I ran back to the couch and watched him back the car off the sidewalk into the street. He sped off burning rubber.

"Who was that?" I asked.

"Bobby Joe and Linda."

"Her name is Linda?"

"Yeah, her name is Linda."

I sat there in disbelief at what I'd witnessed. The girl, the man, and how he just threw her around like a rag doll. Another memory carved in my mind like a bad dream. From then on, a loathing would

come over me every time I'd see a Cadillac
Eldorado.

CHAPTER TWELVE

LAST DAY ADVENTURES

I opened the door to a recognizable sound. Genie Boy's nose had mostly healed.

"You wanna go to the cement yard and check it out?"

Where's the other two?" I asked him.

"Outside," he said.

"I'll be out in a minute."

Mama was on the bed in her room as she often was reading a book. I told her I was going out and would be back soon. She waved me off and went back to reading.

I stepped outside and heard a new song called *Grazing in the Grass* by the Friends of Distinction.

Grazin' in the grass is a gas, baby, can you dig it? What a trip just watchin' as the world goes past. Grazin' in the grass is a gas, baby, can you dig it.

We crossed the street and walked up to a gate with broken pieces of plastic partially woven into the fence. It had two linked gateways with a long chain and lock dangled between the open spaces. The opening was wide enough for a car to go through. Once inside, I looked around, to my left I saw grass growing through silted cement and dirt mixture. A tree leaned against the far back fenced area and to my right was a partial driveway with grass poking through it. There were a run-down rusted building and that odd thing that looked like a steel beehive, as we walked closer, it was above our heads. A long piece of steel extended downward from it like a tube. Water was falling from the end of it; the water fell to the ground like an overhead shower. About the middle way of the ground was a cement yard that was a large pool mixed with cement silt and dirt. The color around the outer edges was dusty gray. The next ring was a darker gray and even darker at its center.

"Hey, look at that pool over there!" Terri said running in the direction of the pool.

"Don't go over there!" Genie Boy shouted. "That stuff is wet! You might...."

But before Genie Boy got the words "fall in," out of his mouth, Terri had gone too far and went down with one plop!

"Terri don't move! Don't move! Stay still!" Genie Boy shouted over and over.

Gary quickly looked around and found a long stick and ran back to the edge of the pool. He plopped the stick down and said, "Hold on, hold on. We'll pull you out."

Gary was first, Genie Boy next and I was last. We pulled as hard as we could and finally the quicksand gave way and released him. Terri looked like he had been breaded in cement.

"Stop playin' around so much." Genie Boy was angry and relieved all at once.

Terri said, "I need to get this stuff off me."

"Are you goin' home?" I asked him.

Why? There's a shower right there," Terri said as he walked under the spilling water letting it drench him. That coated pancake mixture ran right off.

Gary said, "Nothin' like an outside shower."

We were just standing around waiting for Terri to finish his shower when I had an idea, "Y'all wanna go to the Capitol?"

"Why not?" Terri said.

We left without a second thought as Terri dripped dried. Down under the overpass to the large green grassy area with the Capitol in the distance, I ran around and around as fast as my healing ankle allowed. Around and around until I fell on the grass. Genie Boy, Gary and Terri pedaled their bikes like speed racers. Zigzagging around and between one another. They returned to where I was.

"Do you wanna ride?" Terri asked me.

I got on his bike and said, "I'm gettin' on the sidewalk."

I pedaled up the walkway and gained momentum. I felt free as the breeze that blew on my face. Free to be me. Free from hurt and pain. Just for a moment I was free.

Just then I turned around and stopped. A painful thought returned. I had something to tell them. I'd to tell them now. Heading back toward my friends, my heart sank. When I reached the three boys, I sat down, fell back on the grass and gave out a big sigh. Genie Boy suddenly put Terri in a headlock.

Terri said, "Genie Boy, stop playin' around."

"I'm glad you alright. That's all." Genie Boy shared his relief out loud.

"Me too."

Sadness overcame me as I knew my family was leaving for Los Angeles soon.

"Terri, are your pants stiff enough?" I laughed.

"Man, all you need now is a tin spout on your head," Gary chuckled.

Genie Boy stood and started imitating the Tin Man from the "Wizard of Oz" with a stiff-legged dance.

"Ha-ha, y'all so funny I forgot to laugh."

"I do have somethin' to tell you guys," I said breaking the silence that had fallen over our time together.

Genie Boy and Terri did the unison thing again with, "What?"

Gary just sat there silent as he often did.

"My family is going to Los Angeles."

"You are?" Terri exclaimed.

"Yes, we are."

Genie Boy said, "When?"

"Next week."

We all sat there for a moment that seemed to stretch like a lifetime. I broke the silence with, "I'm going home."

"Can I walk with you?" Genie Boy asked smiling at me.

"Sure!"

Terri said, "I'm comin' too.

You comin'?" Genie Boy asked Gary.

"Naw, catch you later."

They walked me down the sidewalk, under the overpass and up to my place. They pedaled off, and I did not think they heard a word of all I said. I walked upstairs and knocked on the door where my little sister was.

"What's wrong with you now?" she asked when she saw my face.

"I told Genie Boy, Gary and Terri we are going to Los Angeles."

"Are you goin' to eat?"

"What? Eat what?" I asked.

"Mama got some lunchmeat and stuff in the kitchen," she said while pointing to the kitchen area. I plopped down on the couch in our close-knit living room.

"Maybe later."

"You know Bruce will vacuum up all that's left. Don't say I didn't tell you."

Memories swirled through my mind, beginning with meeting them just outside my uncle's place, jumping that stupid train and this day with Terri dipped in cement up to his armpits, taking an outdoor shower and looking like the Tin Man from the Wizard of Oz. Ending the day like a whirlwind at the Capitol; it all happened way too fast. Tears slowly streamed along the sides of my face, and I turned my body toward the back of the couch. *I will miss them all.*

"Minnee, wake up, wake up. That Genie Boy is at the door," my sister said shaking me from my nap.

"What? Who?" I asked.

"Your friend, the Genie man, is at the door."

"Okay, okay," waving her off me. I cracked the door.

"You wanna sit outside for a while?"

"Sure, in a minute."

I walked slowly downstairs. Outside, the sky had turned a purplish pink and orange at the horizon. Upward was a deep blue. Looking at Terri, he seemed dusty,

"Hey, Terri, a little itchy?" Gary teased. "Nothin' like a dip in cemented dirt."

"Yeah, "Tin Man style," Genie Boy said.

"Y'all funny, huh?" Terri snarled.

For a moment the awkward silence was back.

"You know up there is the big dipper," Gary said leaning back looking up toward the sky. "I learned people on ships used the end of the handle star as a guide to the North."

"Really?" Terri questioned.

"That's what I learned." Gary said. "I think it's seven stars in the big dipper. Let's look for it."

Genie Boy commented, "There it is. Right there, see the big part looks like a square and the handle bends a little down."

"Where?" Terri asked.

Genie Boy pointed, "Right there. Look straight up."

"I still don't see it."

"Turn away and look up again, where Genie Boy's pointing," Gary instructed.

Terri did what Gary suggested and said, "Still don't see nothin' but stars."

"They are stars," I told him.

Terri said, "Still funny, huh?"

We were all leaning back with arms propped behind our heads at that point. Another moment of silence passed when Gary said, *"I wonder if the stars will look the same in ten years? Will the stars be just like that in ten years?" Hard times, hard times, there would be no times without hard times. Baby dies, Mama lies about desertion. Papa says, 'Mama's baby, Papa's maybe.' Hard times are so shady. 'Kiss me, death,' the beggar man says, funny not that hungry family. Hard times are their misery. Pack of dudes in the way, be careful little bird or you will be swept away. Symbol neck, symbol hands. Can't believe or understand. Let me know. Let me go. I have a hunch; its hard times turn to take a punch. Hard times. Hard times there would be no times without hard times."*

"Is that a poem or something?" I asked.

"Yeah."

"Wow," Terri said impressed by his friend's words.

Genie Boy asked me, "Why are y'all goin' to Los Angeles?"

"I dunno."

"How did you find out?" Terri looked sad as he asked me the question.

"Mama told me in the kitchen."

"Unreal," Terri added.

"What time are y'all leavin'?" Genie Boy said looking all around.

"Early Sunday mornin'."

CHAPTER THIRTEEN

NEVER GONE FOR LONG

Mama, my brother, sister and I didn't have much to take but a few bags of clothes and other stuff. We piled into a small U-Haul truck with our belongings. Bruce and Alice were riding shotgun. I was in disbelief during the entire drive to Los Angeles. Anne arranged for us a place to stay or so it seemed. When we arrived in our new city, we pulled up to an apartment complex. We walked up the long sidewalk leading into an open area with grass, flower bushes and two benches in the center of the space. There were apartments lined around the first and second floors of the garden area with sidewalks forming a rectangle.

We followed Mama around the first level area, turned left and at the second door, we stopped. Mama knocked on the door and Anne opened the door. We walked in, the apartment had a bathroom to the right, kitchen to the left and living room area at the back of the place. It was big enough for one, maybe two people. We stood in the living room area and several sizable paintings were propped around the walls of the living room space. The canvases were made of black and red velvet colors. The drawings were of Afro American women and men and one Panther. A few drawings were men and women embracing. They all had afros. Two particular ones had afro picks in their hair. They were all in their birthday suits. The paint was bright with the that glow-in-the-dark stuff; the artwork was incredible. We left the apartment and walked with Anne up the street to another house. It was about a block away. A block in Los Angeles was longer than a mile. We walked up two flights of stairs to a brown wooden house. We sat in the living room for the rest of the day until night. A woman entered the house and walked into another room with Anne who followed behind her.

"They can't stay here. It's too many of them. They have to leave in the morning," we heard the woman shout at Anne.

Early the next morning, we left walking on what was called *Figueroa Boulevard* in South Central LA. We were without food, without a house, without what we brought with us. The LA sun was so hot. Not that walking in the sun was something we couldn't handle. Mama, Bruce, Alice and I were cross city trekkers. Following Mama, we learned how to navigate a city on foot. Out of nowhere a man walked up to Mama like the superhero, "The Flash" and palmed a fifty-dollar bill in her hand.

"Here! I think you need this," he said.

I was the closest to Mama while we walked. The next stop was a bus stop bench. I sat on that bench and turned my head to the right and the man was gone. *Where did he go? Where did he come from?* I wondered. There were not many people walking that morning. *How did he vanish like that? What chance was it that this man would give Mama fifty dollars? How did he know our circumstances?* We were in Los Angeles for maybe 20 hours. He appeared and disappeared just like that!

Just like that! *Can angels look like people, too?* I know it was divine intervention.

Slightly past the bus stop was a street light. We crossed the street and went to the diner on the corner. Mama ordered us food. I ate meatloaf, but the mashed potatoes tasted like sawdust and the green beans smelled loud like boiled mushrooms. "Yuck!"

Mama had this way about her where she could charm a cat out of a tree. She talked to a lady who sat next to her. Mama talked about our dilemma and it happened that the lady was going to Germany. She was waiting for movers to move her stuff. She lived behind the diner. The lady allowed us to stay in her place even though boxes were all over the living room along with two cats. We played with the cats; one was on the chubby side though.

Mama found a place to stay just two doors down from the diner, atop a record shop. It was an upstairs apartment. After which she obtained a job with NCR; a technology company. Mama worked on some kind of assembly line. We eventually moved to *Compton Boulevard*. This process took about three months. What a relief it was. We had a place to stay, food in the icebox, and we were going to school; how cool was that?

After a year, lo and behold Mama's on-again-off-again boyfriend popped up in Compton and all of us went back to Oklahoma City with him.

My brother, sister and I sat on my great grandmother's couch with long faces. I couldn't believe we had come back after all we had been through in California. There was an undercurrent of emotions that I saw between Mama and Great Grandma. Eventually, we moved to a house off Kelley Avenue on the eastside of the city.

One day I heard a familiar sound at the door and excitement overcame me. I opened the door and there stood Genie Boy and off to the right side of him was Terri. I stepped out on the porch; I couldn't believe my eyes.

"How did y'all find out we was back?" I said happily.

"Bruce told us," Genie Boy said.

"That figures."

I walked to the edge of the porch and sat down. They sat down, too.

"What y'all been doing?" I wanted to know.

Genie Boy said, "Nothin' much. Going to school and all."

"What y'all do in Los Angeles?"

"It was crazy at first. We got to this apartment and it was big enough for two people to live in. We went to this other lady's house, and she put us out. We got a place though later. Mama's boyfriend brought us back. Where's Gary?" I said as I suddenly thought about his absence from the group.

"He's in the Boys' Reformatory," Genie Boy answered.

"The what?"

"He got in trouble for stealin' something."

"Did he have brothers or sisters?"

"Yeah, he had a big sister and one baby sister who died or somethin'."

I asked, "What was his sister's name?"

"You talkin' bout the older one?"

"Yes."

"Linda."

At that moment the scene rolled again in my mind, the girl with the green and glassy eyes, brown freckles on her face and reddish-brown hair with looping curls.

"Linda are you alright?" I remember Anne asking her after the man had thrown her down the flight of stairs.

"You said her name was Linda?" I asked double checking what I had heard.

Genie Boy said, "Yeah. Her name was Linda."

What's the matter with you? You look like you seen a ghost," Terri said.

"I think I met her before."